A very buggy problem!

A young guy wearing a white apron carried a tray of cupcakes past the girls. Nancy guessed he was Trent, the junior baker.

"Just think," George sighed. "Some of those spent the night at my house."

"What a sweet sleepover!" Bess swooned.

Nancy's heart beat faster as they got closer to the counter. Would she try the chocolate one? Or lemon? Or the famous purple passion cupcake? But before Nancy could decide, a loud scream interrupted her thoughts.

"What happened?" Nancy wondered out loud.

More people screamed from the front of the café. Nancy, Bess, and George pushed their way to the counter to see what was up.

That's when Bess screamed too.

"OMG!" Bess cried. "A swarm of ladybugs has invaded the store!"

Join the CLUE CREW
& solve these other cases!

Nancy Drew

AND THE CLUE CREW

#34

Cupcake Chaos

By Carolyn Keene

Illustrated by Macky Pamintuan

Aladdin

New York London Toronto Sydney New Delhi

ALADDIN
An imprint of Simon & Schuster Children's Publishing Division
1230 Avenue of the Americas, New York, NY 10020
First Aladdin paperback edition March 2013
Text copyright © 2013 by Simon & Schuster, Inc.
Illustrations copyright © 2013 by Macky Pamintuan
All rights reserved, including the right of reproduction in whole or in part in any form.
ALADDIN is a trademark of Simon & Schuster, Inc., and related logo is a registered trademark of Simon & Schuster, Inc.
NANCY DREW AND THE CLUE CREW is a registered trademark of Simon & Schuster, Inc.
For information about special discounts for bulk purchases, please contact Simon & Schuster Special Sales at 1-866-506-1949 or business@simonandschuster.com.
The Simon & Schuster Speakers Bureau can bring authors to your live event. For more information or to book an event contact the Simon & Schuster Speakers Bureau at 1-866-248-3049 or visit our website at www.simonspeakers.com.
The text of this book was set in ITC Stone Informal.
Manufactured in the United States of America 0213 OFF
10 9 8 7 6 5 4 3 2 1
Library of Congress Control Number 2012949906
ISBN 978-1-4424-5351-7
ISBN 978-1-4424-5352-4 (eBook)

CONTENTS

ChaPTER ONE

Sneak Peek

"If this is the first week of spring," eight-year-old Nancy Drew said, "why does it still feel like winter?"

Nancy's best friend George Fayne shrugged. "Maybe spring hasn't sprung yet!" she said.

"This is my favorite season!" Bess Marvin, Nancy's other best friend, said with a smile.

"What do you like best about it?" Nancy asked Bess. "Spring flowers? Spring weather—"

"Spring *clothes*!" Bess declared.

Nancy smiled. Outside it was chilly, but inside George's kitchen it was warm and sunny. While George's mom worked in her home office, the three BFFs sipped cocoa around the kitchen table.

"We've got more than the season to celebrate, you guys," George said, licking away a hot-chocolate mustache. "Tomorrow the Lucky Ladybug Cupcake Café opens for business!"

The three friends reached across the table to high-five. Not only would the Lucky Ladybug be the first cupcake bakery on Main Street but the owners, Gwendolyn and Carolyn, were practically superstars!

The Porters were identical twins. They looked alike—and even baked alike!

"Did you see the sisters on that TV show *Cupcake Crusaders*?" Nancy asked. "Their cupcakes look too good to eat!"

"Then I'll keep my eyes closed!" Bess joked.

George smiled slyly as she stood up. "Are you ready for a big secret?" she asked.

"Secret?" Bess said. "Since when do cousins keep secrets from each other?"

"And best friends?" Nancy asked.

"I'm about to tell you, aren't I?" George said. She walked over to the huge steel fridge. Mrs.

2

Fayne was a caterer and needed an extra-big refrigerator for party food.

"Ta-daaa!" George sang as she pulled the door open.

Nancy gave a little gasp. She brushed her reddish blond hair from her eyes so she could make sure what she was seeing was real. . . .

"Lucky Ladybug cupcakes!" Nancy said.

"What are they doing here?" Bess asked.

"My mom is holding the extra cupcakes in

3

her fridge until tomorrow," George said. "As a favor to Gwendolyn and Carolyn."

"I want a taste!" Bess squealed.

"Me too!" Nancy said as she and Bess ran to the fridge.

George's dark curls bounced as she shook her head. "No sneak tastes," she said. "Just sneak peeks."

The girls gazed at the dreamy-looking cupcakes. Nancy's favorites were the cupcakes with the sunflower design. Bess's favorites were the bright purple ones.

"Pink is my favorite color," Bess said, swooning. "But that's the most beautiful purple I've ever seen."

"They're called purple passion cupcakes," George said. "Gwendolyn and Carolyn told me when they loaded the fridge."

Nancy thought the cupcakes looked yummy. But were they the best?

"I wonder if those cupcakes taste as good as Olivia Chow's," Nancy said.

Olivia Chow was in the girls' third-grade class at River Heights Elementary School. Every Saturday she sold her own cupcakes from a table she set up on Main Street.

"There's only one way to find out," Bess said, reaching out her hand.

"What part of 'no' don't you get?" George said. She was about to close the fridge when a voice said, "Don't shut that door, George Fayne!"

Nancy, Bess, and George whirled around. Standing behind them was—

"Deirdre Shannon," Bess groaned.

Eight-year-old Deirdre was spoiled and a bit snooty. She usually got whatever she wanted, including her own blog, called Dishing with Deirdre.

"How did you get in here?" George asked.

"I told your mom I was a reporter," Deirdre said coolly. "And that I want to write about the Lucky Ladybug cupcakes for my blog."

"How did you know we had Lucky Ladybug cupcakes?" George demanded.

"News reporters know everything," Deirdre said.

"You mean gossip girls," Bess muttered.

"Heard that!" Deirdre said.

George stepped in front of Deirdre. "Those cupcakes are a secret until tomorrow," she said.

"How can I write about them if I can't taste them?" Deirdre whined.

"You'll have to wait until tomorrow, like everyone else," Nancy said.

Deirdre turned and stomped loudly out of the kitchen. "You're just jealous," she snapped. "Because I'm a reporter and you're just silly detectives!"

Nancy glanced sideways at Bess and George. They weren't silly detectives—they were awesome detectives. They had their own detective club, called the Clue Crew. They even had cool headquarters in Nancy's room!

"She didn't want a story," Bess said. "Just a free cupcake."

The girls forgot about Deirdre as they gave the treats one last gaze.

"Lucky Ladybug cupcakes in my own kitchen," George sighed. "How's that for lucky?"

"Lucky like a ladybug!" Nancy declared. She couldn't wait for tomorrow—and for the best cupcakes ever!

"Why the superhealthy dinner, Hannah?" Mr. Drew asked. He winked at Nancy across the table. "Is it to make up for all the cupcakes Nancy is going to eat tomorrow?"

Nancy giggled as Hannah Gruen passed around the platter of veggie burgers. Hannah was the Drews' housekeeper and an awesome cook. But she was also more than that. Nancy's own mom had died when Nancy was only three years old, and ever since, Hannah had been like a mother to her.

"You know I like healthy meals," Hannah said with her usual cheery smile. "And now so does Mayor Strong."

"What does the mayor have to do with it?" Nancy asked.

"Mayor Strong wants to make River Heights healthy," Hannah said. "He wants restaurants to cut back on sugar. He even started a jogging club called Running Strong!"

"In that case," Mr. Drew said, "I doubt you'll see Mayor Strong at the Lucky Ladybug Cupcake Café tomorrow."

"Why not, Daddy?" Nancy asked.

Mr. Drew smiled as he poured dressing on his salad. "Cupcakes aren't exactly filled with vitamins, honey," he said.

"Sure they are, Daddy." Nancy giggled. "Vitamin Y for yummy!"

Suddenly Nancy heard a bark. It was her puppy, Chocolate Chip, in the front hallway. She excused herself from the table to check on the pup.

"What's up, Chip?" Nancy asked.

The little chocolate Labrador was pawing the front door. Was somebody outside? Nancy stood on her tiptoes and peeked out the peephole. Nobody there.

"It's probably a squirrel," Nancy decided.

But when she opened the door a crack, she saw no squirrels anywhere. Nancy was about to shut the door when she spotted something strange on the doorstep.

"If that *is* a squirrel, Chip," Nancy said slowly, "it's disguised as a creamy green cupcake."

Nancy looked closer. It *was* a cupcake, with a tiny piece of paper sticking out of the top. Carefully Nancy pulled out the paper and read the message written on it:

DO NOT EAT AT THE LUCKY LADYBUG CUPCAKE CAFE—EVER!

CHAPTER TWO

Bugged Out

"I've heard of fortune cookies," George said the next morning. "But not creepy fortune *cupcakes*."

It was Saturday morning. Nancy and her friends were headed to Main Street for the Lucky Ladybug opening.

Nancy had told the girls about the mysterious cupcake on her doorstep. Bess and George had each received one too!

"I think Deirdre left them," Nancy said. "She was mad at us for not letting her taste the cupcakes yesterday."

"Well, Deirdre Shannon is not keeping us from the Lucky Ladybug today!" George insisted.

Bess flipped her long, blond hair back. "Speaking of ladybugs," she said. "Look at my new earrings."

"They look like big ladybugs!" Nancy said, smiling.

"Only you would find ladybug earrings, Bess," George teased.

Bess planted her hands on her hips. "When are you going to start wearing earrings, George Fayne?" she asked.

"When they're computerized!" George replied.

Nancy giggled. Bess and George were cousins but as different as night and day. Bess loved fashion-forward clothes and accessories. The only accessories George loved were for her computer and MP3 player!

"Let's go," Nancy said. "Or we'll miss the opening ceremony."

"And free cupcakes!" Bess said happily.

Since Main Street was five blocks away, the girls were allowed to walk there. They could walk anywhere together as long as it was five blocks or less from their houses. That was cool, since Nancy, Bess, and George went everywhere together anyway.

"The sisters picked up their cupcakes early this morning," George said as they walked.

"Who was watching the store?" Nancy asked.

"Their junior baker, Trent," George explained. "He was there baking even more cupcakes."

"Bring it!" Bess said happily.

A blast of cold air hit the girls as they turned onto Main Street. It was still too cold for spring, but not too cold for Olivia Chow and her cupcake stand. . . .

"Come and get some cupcakes!" Olivia called.

She was wearing her usual sparkly tiara. That's because everybody called her the cupcake queen. Sitting with Olivia was her little brother and assistant, Lester.

"We've got chocolate, red velvet, and pistachio cream!" Lester shouted. "Check it out!"

"Can't," George said. "We're on our way to—"

Bess jabbed George with her elbow, but it was too late.

"I knew it!" Olivia groaned. "You're on your way to that Bedbug Café!"

"Ladybug," Nancy corrected.

"Those cupcakes are going to put me out of business," Olivia complained.

"And we were going to start serving lemonade, too," Lester groaned. "Three flavors!"

"People will always want your cupcakes, Olivia," Nancy said gently. "It's just that Gwendolyn and Carolyn are—"

"Famous," George finished.

"Big deal!" Olivia snapped. "You won't catch me going into that store. Ever!"

Nancy gazed down at Olivia's cupcakes. The green ones looked exactly like the cupcake on her doorstep last night.

She was about to ask Olivia about them when Bess tugged her arm.

"Come on, Nancy," Bess whispered. "Or we'll miss the opening."

"Did you see Olivia's green cupcakes?" Nancy asked as they walked on. "They looked just like the one on my doorstep last night."

"The cupcake on my doorstep was green too," George said.

"I thought you said Deirdre left those creepy cupcakes, Nancy," Bess said.

"I changed my mind," Nancy said. "If anyone

would want to stop us from eating Lucky Lady-bug cupcakes, it's Olivia."

Bess's eyes widened. "What if Olivia is planning more trouble?" she asked. "Like at the café today?"

Nancy shook her head. "Olivia said she'd never go there," she said. "Ever!"

Nancy, Bess, and George had no trouble finding the Lucky Ladybug. It was the only store with a colorful balloon arch over the door and a crowd of kids out front. There was even a television news crew covering the event!

The girls were happy to see kids from school, like Kendra Jackson and Peter Patino. But *unhappy* to see Deirdre Shannon . . .

Deirdre was rolling her eyes at the tap-dancing kids under the balloon arch. The dancers were dressed as ladybugs with antennae bouncing on their heads.

"The big opening sure is big!" Bess shouted over the music.

"Where's Mayor Strong?" George asked.

"Doesn't he always show up for store openings?"

"Cupcakes aren't healthy enough for Mayor Strong these days," Nancy said.

"Unless they're carrot cupcakes!" Bess giggled.

Nancy smiled when she saw Gwendolyn and Carolyn standing near the balloons. They wore snowy white aprons and baker's hats designed to look like cupcakes. Cool!

"I want to meet them!" Nancy said.

The three friends squeezed through the crowd toward the sisters—until a boy pushed past them.

"Out of my way!" the boy shouted.

"Hey!" George complained as the boy's heavy backpack bumped her.

Nancy, Bess, and George recognized him at once. It was Bobby Wozniak from the fourth grade. Bobby's nickname was Buggy, and for a good reason. He was president of the Bug Club, a club where bug-loving kids met every Sunday. This included Nancy's classmates Sonia Susi and Michael D.

"Now I know why Buggy is president of the Bug Club," George muttered. "He's a pest!"

Buggy had already reached the sisters. Nancy could hear him as he spoke out loud:

"The Bug Club likes that you named your cupcake café after a bug—so we want to hang our poster next to your store."

Buggy held up a handmade poster. Bess gagged. It was a collage of tarantulas, beetles, and even bedbugs!

"I tried using real bugs," Buggy said. "But they kept crawling away."

Gwendolyn stared at the poster. "Um," she said uncomfortably. "That poster isn't quite right for a café."

"There isn't one ladybug on it either," Carolyn said.

"Just the gross kind!" George added.

Buggy scowled as he began to walk away. This time he bumped Nancy with his backpack. Instead of "excuse me," though, Buggy said, "I'll bet the cupcakes in there are gross too!"

"Ouch!" Nancy said as they watched Buggy leave. "What's he carrying in there—rocks?"

"Probably one of his bug farms," George said. "I heard he has dozens of them in his room."

"Too much information!" Bess complained.

Nancy wanted to change the subject from bugs to the café. She turned to the sisters and said, "Are your purple passion cupcakes in the store today?"

"They sure are!" Carolyn said.

"Somebody already ate a few purple passions this morning," Gwendolyn said. "But we don't know who."

"Probably Trent," George whispered as the sisters turned back to the dancers.

The crowd applauded as the dancers finished their show. They applauded even louder for Gwendolyn and Carolyn.

"They say ladybugs are lucky, and we can't think of anything luckier than selling cupcakes right here in River Heights!" Carolyn told everyone.

"My ladybug watch says it's eleven o'clock

on the dot!" Gwendolyn said. "Which means the Lucky Ladybug Cupcake Café is open for business."

"Woo-hooooo!" George cheered.

Nancy, Bess, and George followed the crowd under the balloon arch and through the door. Inside, the smell of sweet cream and sugar wafted up their noses.

A young guy wearing a white apron carried a tray of cupcakes past the girls. Nancy guessed he was Trent, the junior baker.

"Just think," George sighed. "Some of those spent the night at my house."

"What a sweet sleepover!" Bess swooned.

Nancy's heart beat faster as they got closer to the counter. Would she try the chocolate one? Or lemon? Or the famous purple passion cupcake? But before Nancy could decide, a loud scream interrupted her thoughts.

"What happened?" Nancy wondered out loud.

More people screamed from the front of the

café. Nancy, Bess, and George pushed their way to the counter to see what was up.

That's when Bess screamed too.

"OMG!" Bess cried. "A swarm of ladybugs has invaded the store!"

CHAPTER THREE

Unlucky Ladybugs

Nancy screamed too. She liked real, live lady-bugs but not hundreds of them all at once. Especially not all over cupcakes!

"They're only ladybugs, you guys!" George told the crowd as they went wild.

"They're still bugs, George," Bess said. "And bugs are icky!"

"Run for it!" a boy shouted.

"It's raining ladybugs!" one girl cried out.

A bunch of kids charged toward the door.

"Wait!" Gwendolyn called. "There's got to be a good reason for this!"

Not everybody ran out of the bugged-out café. Deirdre stood alone taking pictures of the scene with a bright pink camera. Nancy, Bess, and George stuck close together near the counter.

"Where did all these ladybugs come from?" Nancy said over the noise.

"What if Lucky Ladybug cupcakes are made out of real ladybugs?" Bess cried.

"Some secret recipe that would be," George groaned.

"The sisters do not cook with bugs," Nancy said. "Like they said—there's got to be a reason for this."

A ladybug landed on Nancy's nose and she shrieked. Whatever the reason—it had better be a good one!

George blew the ladybug off her friend's nose. Then the three friends hurried over to Gwendolyn and Carolyn. The sisters were frantically swatting ladybugs while talking to the news reporter.

"Ladybug Café . . . real ladybugs," the reporter said. "Did you do this for the publicity?"

"Absolutely not!" Gwendolyn insisted.

Also swatting ladybugs was Trent. The junior baker looked even more upset than the sisters.

Suddenly Deirdre Shannon pushed past the girls to Gwendolyn and Carolyn.

"Deirdre Shannon of my very own blog, Dishing with Deirdre," she said. "I have some questions for you."

"Excuse me, young lady," the news reporter

cut in. "We were conducting an interview."

"So am I," Deirdre snapped. She shoved what looked like a voice recorder under Carolyn's chin. "Is it true you stored your cupcakes somewhere else last night?"

Before Carolyn could answer, Deirdre pointed her finger at George. "Like at the Fayne house?" she demanded.

"Are you blaming my mom for all these ladybugs?" George said angrily.

"Your mom or you," Deirdre said. "You always are joking . . . *Georgia* Fayne."

Nancy and Bess gulped as George's face turned tomato red. Nobody used her real name and got away with it!

"Please, everybody leave," Gwendolyn said. "So we can take care of this problem."

Kendra and Peter were still in the store too.

"Does that mean we won't get cupcakes?" Kendra asked.

"We can spit out the ladybugs," Peter suggested. "No big deal."

"There will be no cupcakes until we reopen," Carolyn announced.

"If we reopen," Gwendolyn muttered.

Deirdre and the news crew refused to leave. So did Nancy. She still had no clue how live ladybugs ended up in the café, but she was determined to find out.

Nancy waved her friends to the side. George was the first to start whispering.

"The news camera was on all that time,"

George hissed. "Thanks to Deirdre, everyone will know my real name—and think my house is crawling with bugs!"

"Not if we find the real reason this happened," Nancy whispered.

"But it's a mystery," Bess said.

"Exactly," Nancy said with a smile. "A mystery means another case for the Clue Crew."

The girls exchanged a quiet high five. They were about to start looking for clues when Bess pointed to a half-opened door in the back.

"Look!" Bess said. "There's a pretty garden out there."

Through the door Nancy could see green bushes and bright yellow daffodils.

"Come on!" Bess said as she darted toward the back.

"What is she doing?" George complained. "We don't have time to sniff flowers."

Nancy made sure no one was looking. Then she and George slipped out the back door after Bess.

Once they stepped outside, their jaws dropped. Not only were there daffodils and other flowers, there were outdoor tables and chairs. A white wooden fence surrounded the whole place.

"An outdoor café!" Nancy said with a smile. "For when the weather gets warmer."

"If it ever gets warmer," George said. "Let's go inside before the sisters find us here."

"Not until we smell the pretty flowers," Bess said. "Come on, Nancy!"

Nancy followed Bess to a patch of tiny green ones. The marker was still stuck in the ground.

"Those are *Eranthis . . . hyemalis*," Nancy said.

Bess pointed to a cluster of white flowers sprouting from a bush. "I think these are called snowdrops," she said excitedly. "They smell awesome."

As Nancy sniffed the fragrant blooms she heard George's voice: "I think I found another bug."

"A ladybug?" Nancy asked, looking up.

"A *litter* bug," George said. She held up

an empty glass jar. "Somebody dropped this between some bushes."

George was about to toss the jar into a trash can when Nancy noticed the label.

"Let me see that, please," Nancy said.

George handed Nancy the jar. As she read the label, her eyes flew wide open.

"What was in the jar, Nancy?" Bess asked.

"Ladybugs," Nancy said. "Five hundred *live* ladybugs!"

CHAPTER FOUR

Cupcake Clues

"I didn't know ladybugs came in jars just like peanut butter!" Bess exclaimed.

"Me neither," Nancy admitted. "But we now know where those ladybugs came from."

"But the jar wasn't in the store," George said. "It was out here in the garden."

"Whoever dumped the ladybugs must have run out the back door into the garden," Nancy said. "Then he or she got rid of the jar—"

"Then climbed over the fence and got away!" George cut in.

"Aren't you glad I wanted to come back here?" Bess asked excitedly. "Well, aren't you?"

"Yes, Bess," George groaned.

Nancy slipped the jar into her bag. "This is a very good clue," she said. "Now all we need are some good suspects."

Gwendolyn, Carolyn, and Trent were still swatting ladybugs as Nancy, Bess, and George left through the front door. As the girls walked up Main Street, they passed Olivia's cupcake stand and a long line of kids. Unlike before, business was booming!

"Try my rocky road cupcakes!" Olivia called to the kids. "They rock!"

"At least somebody is happy about those ladybugs," Bess said quietly.

When the Clue Crew reached the Drew house, they went straight up to Nancy's room. George immediately sat down at the computer.

"What do we know so far?" George said, her fingers flying across the keyboard.

"We know someone dumped real, live ladybugs in the Lucky Ladybug Cupcake Café," Nancy said.

Bess sat on Nancy's bed. She gazed at the empty ladybug jar in her hands. "Wow," she said. "Think of all the good luck you'd get from five hundred ladybugs."

"They weren't lucky for Gwendolyn and Carolyn," Nancy said.

George pointed to the computer screen. "I found a whole bunch of sites for ordering live bugs," she said.

Nancy took the jar from Bess and flipped it

over. On the bottom was a label with the name of a bug company.

"These ladybugs came from Pests R Best," Nancy said. "See if they have a website, George."

George quickly found the site. The Pests R Best home page had images of real bugs crawling across it.

"Totally gross!" Bess cried.

"Totally buggy!" George laughed.

Buggy? Nancy's eyes lit up at the word.

"Buggy Wozniak!" Nancy exclaimed. "He was mad at the sisters when they wouldn't let him hang up his poster."

"The jar could have been inside his backpack," George said. "Maybe that's why it was so heavy."

"I'll bet Buggy dumped those ladybugs," Bess declared. "Write that down, George!"

George started the suspect list with Buggy Wozniak. But for the Clue Crew, one suspect was never enough.

"What about Olivia?" Bess asked. "She was

afraid everybody would go to the Lucky Ladybug instead of her cupcake stand."

"Did you see all those kids at Olivia's cupcake stand?" George asked. "I'd say she had a motive."

A motive was a reason for committing the crime. But Nancy wasn't sure about Olivia.

"We saw Olivia at her cupcake stand right before the big opening," Nancy said. "She told us she'd never go to the Lucky Ladybug. Ever!"

George did another search. This time she pulled up Deirdre Shannon's blog, Dishing with Deirdre.

"I knew it!" George cried angrily. "Deirdre wrote about the ladybug swarm and about me!"

"What did she write?" Nancy asked.

"She wrote that some of the cupcakes were stored at a caterer's house," George said. "A caterer whose daughter has the same name as a state."

"Don't worry, George," Bess said gently. "Not everyone knows that your real name is—"

"Don't say it!" George snapped.

Nancy pointed to Deirdre's blog. "She posted a picture of the ladybug swarm too," she said.

The Clue Crew studied the picture. It showed a mob of frantic kids running toward the door.

"I've seen enough," George muttered. She was about to close the site when—

"Wait!" Nancy said. She pointed to the first kid at the door. A boy with dark hair. "Can you make that kid in the picture bigger, George?"

"Easy-peasy, lemon-squeezy," George said. With a single click she enlarged the picture.

"Just as I thought," Nancy said. "It's Lester Chow."

"What does that mean, Nancy?" Bess asked.

"It means one of the Chows *was* inside the Lucky Ladybug Cupcake Café today," Nancy said. "But it wasn't Olivia."

It was Lester!

ChaPTER FiVE

Pest Test

"Olivia probably sent Lester to dump the lady-bugs," George said.

"Maybe she made him leave the creepy cupcakes on our doorsteps too," Bess said.

Nancy stared at the picture. All she could see was Lester's head above the crowd.

"I can't see if he's carrying a backpack or a bag," Nancy said, "to hold the ladybug jar."

"He was in the store when the ladybugs broke loose," George said as she added Lester's name to the suspect list. "That's enough for me."

Nancy asked George to print out the picture. She folded it neatly and slipped it inside her pocket. It was time to start working on the case, but first she had to walk her puppy, Chocolate Chip.

Once outside, the girls headed to the park with Chip. But the little brown puppy had other plans.

"Where is she taking us?" Nancy said as Chip tugged at her leash.

"She's leading us to Main Street," George said.

"Why Main Street?" Bess wondered.

When they reached Main Street, Nancy saw why. Chip was tugging in the direction of Olivia Chow's cupcake stand.

"Listen up!" Olivia called out to the long line of kids. "We're short on red velvet cupcakes, so only one to a customer!"

Lester was behind the table too, pulling cupcakes out of a big plastic bin.

"How did Chip know to bring us to one of our suspects?" Bess asked.

"Chip sniffed one of Olivia's cupcakes last night," Nancy explained. "She must have remembered the scent."

"Good girl, Chip!" George declared.

"Woof!" Chip barked. She still strained at her leash, but Nancy held it tightly.

"Let's question Olivia," Nancy said. "If we can get her away from her cupcakes."

The kids in line grumbled as Nancy, Bess, and George walked straight to the table with Chip.

"I don't want dog hairs on my cupcake!" one girl complained.

"And quit jumping the line!" a boy shouted.

"We're not jumping the line," George told them. "We just want to talk to the cupcake queen."

"Who has time to talk?" Olivia said happily. "Thanks to those ladybugs, my cupcake stand is rocking out!"

"Oh, really?" Bess asked.

"Tell us about the ladybugs, Olivia," George said. "And how Lester dumped a whole jar of them inside the Lucky Ladybug."

Lester was too busy selling cupcakes to hear. But Olivia's eyes flew open. She turned to her brother and said, "Hold the fort, I'll be right back."

"On it, sis!" Lester said with a little salute.

Olivia and the Clue Crew stepped away from the table and the cupcake-hungry crowd.

"So what do you want to know?" Olivia asked.

Nancy needed two hands to hold Chip's leash. So George pulled the picture out of Nancy's pocket.

"We have proof that your brother was at the Lucky Ladybug this morning," George said.

"So?" Olivia said. "I sent Lester there to pick up some cupcakes."

"But you bake your own cupcakes," Bess said.

"Exactly!" Olivia said. "That's why I wanted to taste the competition."

"Huh?" George said.

Olivia rolled her eyes as if to say *Duh!*

"I wanted to see if their cupcakes were better than mine," she explained. "So I sent Lester there to pick up a few."

"That's all?" Nancy asked.

Olivia nodded. "I heard some of them had sprinkles shaped like hearts and daisies," she said.

"Did Lester *sprinkle* some ladybugs on the cupcakes while he was there?" George demanded.

"Lester would never do that," Olivia insisted.

"Why not?" Bess asked.

"He's totally scared of bugs!" Olivia replied. She began counting on her fingers. "Spiders, ants, beetles—"

"Ladybugs?" Nancy cut in.

"Especially ladybugs," Olivia said. "Lester

40

says the little black dots look like more bugs."

Olivia leaned over to whisper, "Just seeing a bug makes him flip. But don't tell him I told you, okay?"

The Clue Crew stared at Olivia as she walked back to her cupcake stand.

"Do you think Olivia was telling the truth about Lester?" Nancy asked.

"I know how we can find out," George said. She held out her hand and said, "Give me one of your earrings, Bess."

"Why?" Bess asked.

"You'll see!" George said impatiently.

Bess looked worried as she handed one of her ladybug earrings to George.

"Now follow me," George said.

The girls and Chip walked back to the cupcake stand. This time they stood behind Olivia and Lester as they sold cupcakes.

"We just unpacked double-chocolate-chip cupcakes, people," Olivia shouted out. "Get 'em while they're yummy!"

George waited until Lester wasn't looking. Then she quickly dropped Bess's earring on the table.

Nancy smiled to herself. So *that* was George's plan—to see if Bess's earring bugged Lester!

"Nice-looking cupcakes you've got there, Lester," George said coolly.

Lester's eyes were still on the customers as he said, "Thanks."

"Too bad there's a *big, fat bug* right next to them!" George blurted.

Lester dropped the cupcake he was holding. "Bug?" he squeaked. "Did you say 'bug'?"

In a blink Lester pulled off his sneaker. He began thumping it on the table in the direction of the earring.

"Die!!" Lester screamed. "Die, miserable bug!"

Kids shrieked as cupcakes flew off the table and into the air. Nancy shrieked too. Soon Olivia's colorful and creamy cupcakes were splattered all over the sidewalk. The only thing left on the table was Bess's ladybug earring.

"Ahhh!" Lester screamed. He was about to bring his sneaker down on the earring when Bess snatched it just in time.

"Nooooooo!" Bess cried.

Shoppers on Main Street were stopping to stare at the demolished cupcakes on the sidewalk. Olivia's mouth hung open in shock. Then suddenly—

"Woof!" Chip barked as she lunged toward the splattered cupcakes. Nancy pulled Chip back, but the damage was already done.

"I told you Lester was scared of bugs!" Olivia shouted at the girls. "Now my cupcakes are ruined and it's your fault!"

Nancy looked sideways at her friends and gulped.

Oops.

ChaPTER Six

Explain the Stain

"Um . . . it's just an earring," Bess told Olivia. "I must have dropped it on the table."

"We can help you clean up the mess if you'd like," Nancy said gently.

"Thanks, but you've done enough," Olivia said.

Lester pointed to the earring in Bess's hand. "That totally looked like a bug to me," he said. "Sure glad it wasn't!"

With Chip in tow, Nancy, Bess, and George left the demolished cupcake stand. As they walked up Main Street, Bess said, "I guess Lester really was scared of bugs."

"You think?" George said.

Nancy stopped walking as she suddenly remembered something. She took out the picture of Lester and the charging crowd.

"This shows Lester leaving by the front door," Nancy pointed out. "Not the back, where we found the ladybug jar."

"Another reason Lester is clean," George said.

"He may be clean," Bess said. "But my ladybug earring is covered with sticky cupcake cream."

Nancy and her friends walked Chip past the Lucky Ladybug Cupcake Café. A sign on the door read CLOSED.

"They will open again!" Nancy said, determined. "As soon as we find out the reason for all those ladybugs."

The girls next headed to the park, as planned. While Chip sniffed an acorn Nancy saw a group of runners. Leading the group was Mayor Strong.

"That must be the mayor's running group," Nancy said. "Hannah told me all about it."

"I wonder if the mayor knows what happened at the Lucky Ladybug," George said.

The other joggers sprinted by, but Mayor Strong stopped to pet Chip. He was dressed in light gray sweats and white sneakers.

"Hi, girls," Mayor Strong said. "Still pretty chilly for spring, eh?"

Nancy nodded. "Do you like to run, Mayor Strong?" she asked.

"You bet, Nancy!" Mayor Strong said. "There's nothing like exercise to keep the mind sharp and body strong."

Nancy could see Bess staring at the mayor with huge eyes. What was up?

"And now's your chance to join in, girls!" Mayor Strong boomed.

"Join in?" Bess repeated.

"Your gym teacher Mr. Wilson and I are having a jumping jacks marathon just for kids tomorrow," Mayor Strong explained. "It's all part of my Make River Heights Healthy plan!"

"Gym class on a Sunday?" George said.

"Mr. Wilson will lead the jumping jacks on

my lawn at one o'clock," Mayor Strong said. "So what do you say?"

Nancy liked doing jumping jacks—but the girls had to jump on the case they were working on!

"Sounds like fun," Nancy said. "But the Clue Crew is busy working on a new case."

"What case?" Mayor Strong said.

"The case of the Lucky Ladybug Cupcake Café," George said. "You did hear what happened there today, didn't you?"

The mayor's smile turned into a frown. He began blinking quickly. Beads of sweat popped up all over his forehead.

"C-c-cupcakes?" Mayor Strong stammered. "Did you say 'cupcakes'?"

Nancy nodded slowly. What was wrong with Mayor Strong?

"I know nothing about the Lucky Ladybug Cupcake Café!" Mayor Strong blurted. "I never eat cupcakes!"

Chip barked as Mayor Strong ran to catch up with his group.

"I never eat cookies!" the mayor called over his shoulder as he ran. "Or doughnuts! Or candy . . ."

Mayor Strong's voice trailed off as he ran on.

"That was weird," Nancy said.

"Totally," George said.

"Something else was weird," Bess said. "Did you see that stain on the mayor's hoodie?"

"Only you would notice a stain, Bess," George said.

"It wasn't just a stain," Bess said. "It was purple. The same color as the purple passion cupcakes."

"But we didn't see the mayor at the Lucky Ladybug today, Bess," George said.

Nancy thought for a minute. Just because they didn't see Mayor Strong didn't mean he wasn't there!

"My dad once told me the mayor has keys to every store on Main Street," Nancy said. "In case of emergencies."

"Mayor Strong probably has one for the Lucky Ladybug, too," Bess said. "He could have used it to get inside before the store opened."

"Wouldn't Trent or the sisters have seen all those ladybugs once they got to the store?" George asked.

"Unless the mayor dumped them in a corner somewhere," Nancy decided, "and they swarmed all over the place because of the crowd."

"But why would Mayor Strong want to do something bad to the Lucky Ladybug?" George asked.

"Mayor Strong doesn't think cupcakes are healthy enough," Nancy explained. "He might have wanted the store to close."

"And while he was dumping ladybugs," Bess added. "He bumped into a purple passion cupcake."

"I guess that explains the stain," Nancy said.

"Too bad we can't search Mayor Strong's house for more clues," George said.

"Who says we can't?" Nancy asked.

"Because he's the mayor, Nancy," Bess said. "Not everybody is invited to his house."

"Until tomorrow," Nancy said with a grin. "Jumping jacks, anyone?"

"Thanks for driving us, Hannah," Nancy said the next day.

"No problem!" Hannah said cheerily. "I'm happy you girls are getting a little exercise."

It was Sunday, shortly before one o'clock. Nancy and the girls sat in the backseat of Hannah's car, each wearing sneakers for jumping jacks. Bess was dressed in pink-and-silver sweats with a matching ponytail holder.

Hannah turned the car into Mayor Strong's driveway and said, "Here we are!"

Nancy, Bess, and George looked out the car window. Mayor Strong and his wife lived in a huge yellow house. Today the front lawn was filled with kids doing jumping jacks. Leading them was Mr. Wilson, a whistle around his neck.

"Come on, kids!" Mr. Wilson was shouting. "Let's see you work up a good sweat!"

Mayor Strong and his wife were doing their best to keep up with Mr. Wilson and the kids. The mayor was wearing the same hoodie with the purple clue.

"Doesn't he ever change his clothes?" Bess whispered.

"Not as often as you, Bess!" George teased.

The girls thanked Hannah as they climbed out of the car. Then they walked across the lawn to join the other jumpers.

Nancy, Bess, and George headed to the back of the crowd so they could talk about the case. They fell in step with the jumping jacks, scissoring their arms and legs.

"The mayor and his wife are doing jumping jacks," Nancy said, flapping her arms in the air. "Who'll let us in the house?"

George huffed and puffed from the exercise. "The Strongs have a housekeeper," she said. "I know because my mom catered a party here once."

Suddenly the mayor stopped jumping and turned around. His wife and Mr. Wilson didn't seem to notice as he slipped through a side door into the house.

"Great," George said. "How can we search the house with the mayor inside?"

"I guess we'll have to wait," Nancy said.

"I can't wait," Bess said as she stopped jumping.

"Why not?" Nancy asked.

"Because I have to go to the bathroom, that's why!" Bess said.

"Couldn't you have done that before you left your house, Bess?" George said.

"Now you sound like my dad," Bess complained.

Still doing jumping jacks, the girls made their way around the house to the front door.

"We can stop jumping now!" George said once they were on the doorstep.

Nancy rang the doorbell. After a few seconds a woman with short, blond hair opened the door. She was wearing a black dress with a white collar and cuffs.

"Don't tell me, let me guess," the housekeeper said. "You want to use the bathroom."

"Yes, please!" Bess said.

The housekeeper waved the girls inside and pointed down a long hallway. "Use the one at the end of the hall," she said. "It's right past the mayor's office."

"Thank you," Bess said. She turned to Nancy and George. "Help me find it."

The girls hurried down the hall. They passed the mayor's office and glanced inside. Sitting on the rug was the mayor's bulldog, Duncan. The dog was licking his chops as he gazed up at Mayor Strong, sitting behind a desk.

Nancy was sure the mayor didn't see them. He was too busy unwrapping a jumbo candy bar!

"That's weird," Nancy whispered. "The mayor said he doesn't eat candy."

Nancy, Bess, and George scurried to the side of the door and peeked inside. Mayor Strong was smiling to himself as he chomped into the candy bar.

"If only we could search the mayor's office for clues," George whispered.

"If only I could go to the bathroom!" Bess wailed.

"Shh," Nancy whispered. "I don't want him to know we're snooping!"

Too late.

Duncan's jowls jiggled as he turned toward the door. Then with a loud bark he charged straight toward the girls!

"Busted," George groaned. "By a bulldog!"

ChaPTER SEVEN

Bird Brained

Duncan stopped at the girls' feet. He began chewing playfully at the hem of Bess's pants.

"Ewww!" Bess cried. "Dog drool!"

The sound of the mayor's voice made Nancy, Bess, and George jump.

"What's the matter, Duncan? Is anyone out there?"

Duncan yapped as he followed the girls into the room. When the mayor saw them he froze with the candy bar in his hand.

"Hi, Mayor Strong," Nancy said.

Mayor Strong looked at the candy bar and gulped. "I—I was just getting rid of this."

He tossed the candy on his desk, then stood up to quiet Duncan.

The girls glanced down as they noticed something fall off the desk. It was a key! It looked brand-new, with a tag hanging from it.

Nancy tilted her head to read it: *Lucky Ladybug Cupcake Café*! That wasn't all. The tag was smudged with a bright purple stain.

"A key to the Lucky Ladybug *and* a purple

passion smudge," George said. "That's proof that the mayor was in the cupcake café!"

"Cupcake?" the mayor said.

Nancy looked up. The mayor was staring at them. Duncan had stopped barking. He was staring at them too.

"I never eat cupcakes!" Mayor Strong said. "Just like I never eat . . . um . . . candy bars."

George held up the key. "Then how do you explain this?" she asked.

"I have keys to all the stores in River Heights," Mayor Strong explained. "A young baker named Trent gave me the Lucky Ladybug's before the store opened yesterday."

"So you didn't sneak into the Lucky Lady-bug?" Nancy asked.

"Definitely not," Mayor Strong insisted. "After Trent gave me the key, he told me to check out their freshly baked cupcakes."

A slow smile came over the mayor's face as he said, "Trent went out to the garden, and I had all those cupcakes to myself . . . to check out."

"That's all you did?" Nancy asked.

Mayor Strong's eyes popped wide open. Beads of sweat began dotting his forehead.

"I did do something else," Mayor Strong said. "Something I'm not very proud of."

Nancy, Bess, and George exchanged excited glances. Was Mayor Strong about to confess to dumping the ladybugs?

"Tell us what you did, Mayor Strong," Bess urged. "Please!"

"I . . . I," Mayor Strong stammered. He then took a deep breath and blurted out, "I ate them!!"

Nancy, Bess, and George stared at Mayor Strong.

"You ate the ladybugs?" Bess cried.

"I ate the *cupcakes*!" Mayor Strong wailed.

"Say what?" George asked.

"My head said no, but my sweet tooth said yes!" Mayor Strong explained. "So I ate one . . .

or two . . . maybe three. And they were delicious!"

"Were they purple passion cupcakes?" Nancy asked.

"How did you know?" Mayor Strong asked, surprised.

As Bess pointed to the stain on the mayor's hoodie, Nancy remembered what Gwendolyn and Carolyn had told them.

Some of the purple passion cupcakes were missing yesterday morning. The girls thought it was Trent. It was really Mayor Strong!

"But, Mayor Strong," Nancy said. "Everyone thinks you're such a health nut."

"That's why I couldn't let anyone know," Mayor Strong said, his eyes wide. "Not even my wife."

Nancy felt bad for Mayor Strong. He didn't want to destroy the Lucky Ladybug. All he wanted to do was eat a few cupcakes.

"My housekeeper, Hannah, likes healthy food too," Nancy said with a smile. "She also says there's nothing wrong with a little treat once in a while."

The mayor seemed to think about it. Then he smiled too. "I agree with Hannah," he said. "That's why I want the Lucky Ladybug to reopen as soon as they're bug free."

"Really?" Bess asked excitedly.

"Truly!" Mayor Strong declared. He gave the girls a little wink. "And from now on when I eat a cupcake or candy bar . . . I'll be a little less sneaky about it."

Duncan agreed with a loud "Roof!"

The girls thanked Mayor Strong, then left his office.

"I guess we can finally rule him out," Nancy said.

"And I can finally go to the bathroom!" Bess sighed.

The jumping jacks marathon was over by the time the girls walked outside. While they waited for Hannah they discussed the case.

"We only have one suspect left," Nancy said. "Buggy Wozniak."

"We'd better question him next," George said.

When Hannah arrived she agreed to drop them off at Buggy's house. As they stood outside, Nancy noticed a bug-shaped sign nailed to a tree.

"'Next Bug Club Meeting Monday, four p.m.,'" Nancy read out loud. "'New Club Members Welcome.'"

"Who would want to join a club like that?" Bess asked.

"We should!" Nancy said. "So we can get into Buggy's room and look for clues."

"What about all those icky bugs?" Bess cried.

"Who says bugs are icky?" a voice asked.

Whirling around, the girls saw Buggy. He was tossing some flattened boxes onto the curb for recycling.

"Can we ask you something, Buggy?" Nancy said.

"Nope," Buggy said. "My mom wants me to clean my room."

With that, Buggy darted into the house.

"Phooey!" Nancy said. "I was just going to ask him about Pests R Best."

"You don't have to," George said. She pointed to the top box in the pile. Stamped on it were the words: PESTS R BEST!

ChaPTeR EiGhT

Bug Thugs

Nancy pointed to a label on the box. "Look!" she said. "It was sent to Bobby Wozniak."

"That proves he orders stuff from Pests R Best!" George declared. "He's probably their biggest customer."

"That does it," Nancy said with a nod. "We're going to that meeting after school tomorrow."

"But Buggy's room is going to be full of bugs!" Bess wailed. "Whether he cleans it or not!"

"So what?" George said. "It's not like you have to touch them."

"Ewww!" Bess cried.

"We have to act and look like bug lovers,"

Nancy suggested. "I have a polo shirt with a grasshopper on the pocket."

"I have a T-shirt with black-and-yellow bumblebee stripes," George said. "What are you going to wear, Bess?"

"Bug spray!" Bess groaned.

That night all Nancy wanted to do was hang out in front of the TV. As she switched channels, she found a show for kids called *Creature Teacher*.

"Something bugging you?" the host of the show said with a big smile. "Good, because today our show is about bugs, bugs, and more bugs!"

"As if I won't see enough bugs tomorrow." Nancy chuckled to herself.

Watching the show, Nancy learned some things about bugs that she never knew before— like some bugs help gardens grow by eating pests called aphids. And just like bears, some bugs hibernate, crawling inside when the weather gets cold.

"Wow," Nancy said.

"Nancy, mind if I watch my basketball game now?" Mr. Drew asked as he came into the den.

"Sure, Daddy," Nancy said, handing him the remote. She'd had enough bugs for one day— but what she learned from the Creature Teacher was pretty cool!

The next day at school Nancy tried to concentrate on math, social studies, and spelling, but her thoughts were filled with the Bug Club. Would they find lots of clues in Buggy's room? Or just lots of *bugs*?

After school the girls rushed home to change. They then met in front of Buggy's house at four o'clock sharp.

"Okay, Clue Crew," Nancy said. "Ready for our first Bug Club meeting?"

"Our first and hopefully our last!" Bess said.

"Remember," Nancy said as she rang the Wozniaks' doorbell. "Don't say anything bad about bugs."

The door was opened by Buggy. He and the other club members were wearing club T-shirts and bouncy antennae on their heads.

"We want to join the Bug Club!" Nancy told Buggy with a smile.

Mona Nash, from the fourth grade, peered over Buggy's shoulder at the girls. "I thought you were detectives," she said.

"Detectives can like bugs too," George said.

Nancy nodded as she pointed to the grass-hopper design on her pocket.

"I thought you said bugs were icky!" Buggy said.

"Um," Nancy blurted. "What we really said is . . . bugs are *quickie!*"

"That's why we can never catch the ones we want!" George added. "Right, Bess?"

"Right," Bess mumbled.

Buggy stepped back to whisper to the others. He then turned toward the girls and said, "Okay. Come with us to my room."

It worked! The Clue Crew followed the Bug

Club up the stairs to Buggy's room.

"Whoa!" George said as they stepped inside.

Buggy's room was filled with bug farms, bug dioramas, and jars filled with live bugs. There was even a glass tank holding a big, hairy tarantula!

Bess looked at the spider and cried, "Icky!"

"Um—she means *sticky!*" Nancy blurted. "What a sticky web that huge spider must weave!"

"That's nothing," Buggy said excitedly. "Our goal is to catch the biggest bug in the whole world."

"So what do you do at meetings?" George asked.

Michael D. shrugged and said, "We build bug farms . . . talk about bugs we saw on TV or under our sinks." He was holding a cage with his pet hissing cockroach, Edgar.

"But today is initiation day!" Sonia said excitedly.

"Initiation?" Nancy repeated.

"If you want to join the Bug Club, you have to pass a test," Buggy explained.

The girls traded worried looks.

"What kind of test?" George asked.

"A guessing game!" Mona said.

Buggy held out three cards, facedown. "Pick a bug card," he told Nancy, Bess, and George. "The one who picks the caterpillar card goes first."

Nancy picked a card and flipped it over. The bug looked like some kind of beetle. George went next, picking a red ant.

"Bess got the caterpillar!" Buggy said, holding up the last card.

"So . . . now what?" Bess asked.

In a flash a club member was behind Bess, tying a bandanna around her eyes.

"I thought this was a guessing game!" Bess complained.

"It is," Buggy said. "You've got to guess the bug we put in your hand."

"In my hand?" Bess cried.

Stunned, Nancy stared at George. This wasn't the guessing game she was expecting!

Mona lifted the big, fat tarantula out of the tank. She snickered as she began tiptoeing over to Bess.

"Nancy, Bess is going to flip!" George hissed.

"I know, I know!" Nancy whispered back. "We have to do something. Fast!"

CHAPTER NINE

Top Secret Call

"Let it be a ladybug!" Bess hoped out loud. "Or a pretty butterfly!"

Mona was about to drop the tarantula into Bess's hand when Nancy blurted out: "Too bad that bug isn't as huge as the one we saw in your yard."

All eyes turned to Nancy.

"What kind of bug?" Buggy asked.

"Er . . . we weren't sure," George said. "But he was about the size of my foot."

Excited whispers filled the room.

"That must be the biggest bug in the world!" Buggy exclaimed.

"Bugzilla—at last!" Michael D. declared.

Nancy pointed out the window. "Bugzilla was crawling near your club sign," she said. "If you hurry, you might catch him."

The Bug Club shot out of Buggy's room. Nancy raced straight to Bess and yanked off her blindfold.

"Let's look for clues before they come back!" Nancy said.

It was all systems go. Nancy peered into the dioramas and bug farms looking for ladybugs. Bess wrinkled her nose as she searched the jars.

George was looking at Buggy's desk when she came across an order form from Pests R Best. "Should we call them?" she asked excitedly.

George reached for a phone on Buggy's desk. She punched in the phone number, then switched on the speaker, so Nancy and Bess could hear everything.

"Hello?" George said into the phone. "This is Buggy—I mean, Bobby—Wozniak calling about my ladybug order."

"Hi, Bobby," the man on the other end said. "Let me pull up your past orders. . . . Hmmm, I'm looking at your history and you never ordered ladybugs."

"He didn't? I mean—I didn't?" George asked.

"I see orders for stinkbugs, cockroaches, milli-pedes," the man said. "Definitely no ladybugs."

"Did you ever deliver ladybugs to River Heights?" George asked.

"Yes," the man said. "But I can't give you that information because it's private."

George thanked the man and hung up.

"Maybe Buggy ordered the ladybugs from another company," she said.

"But the label on the jar said Pests R Best," Nancy said. Suddenly—

"Eeek!!" Bess screamed.

Bess pointed to the floor. Nancy screamed too. Scurrying toward them with long, hairy legs was the tarantula!

"Mona must have dropped it before she ran out of the room!" George said.

Bess screamed again as the spider scampered between her feet.

"What are you doing?" a voice demanded.

Nancy turned to see Buggy and the Bug Club filing into the room. They looked mad.

"There was no Bugzilla out there," Mona said. She coolly picked up the tarantula and placed it back in the tank.

"What are you doing behind my desk?" Buggy asked George.

"Trying to find out who dumped those ladybugs at the cupcake café yesterday," George said.

"You thought I did it?" Buggy said.

"You *were* mad at Gwendolyn and Carolyn," Nancy said. "You also had a huge backpack—big enough to hold a jar of ladybugs."

"That wasn't in my backpack!" Buggy insisted. "I was carrying a birthday present."

"Birthday present?" Nancy repeated.

"After I left the Lucky Ladybug, I went straight to Michael's birthday party," Buggy said.

Michael pointed to a party invitation on Buggy's bulletin board and said, "Check it out!"

Nancy, Bess, and George inspected the invitation closely.

"The party started at eleven o'clock," George whispered. "The same time the Lucky Ladybug Café opened."

"It was a surprise party too," Nancy pointed out. "That means Buggy had to be there on time."

"Maybe somebody else in this club dumped the ladybugs," Bess said loud enough for the others to hear.

"*Everybody* here came to my party," Michael insisted. "The theme was bugs."

"Surprise, surprise," George sighed.

Nancy was pretty sure Buggy was innocent. He had an alibi—proof he was somewhere else at the time of the crime.

"I guess we'll go now," Nancy told the club.

"Not until Bess guesses the bug!" Mona said. She pointed to the tarantula inside the tank. "Go ahead, Bess. What kind of bug is that?"

"The icky kind!" Bess replied. "And I don't mean quickie or sticky!"

Nancy, Bess, and George couldn't leave the Bug Club fast enough.

"All that trouble and not one ladybug," George said as they walked away from the Wozniak house.

"I saw a show about bugs last night," Nancy said. "Did you know that some bugs are used in gardens to eat pests?"

"We were in a garden yesterday," Bess said.

"Some bugs don't like the cold either," Nancy

said. "When it gets too cold they crawl inside."

"It was really cold yesterday," George said.

Nancy stopped walking. Garden . . . cold? Why hadn't she thought of that before?

"Maybe ladybugs eat pests," Nancy said excitedly. "Maybe Gwendolyn and Carolyn used them in their garden and because it was cold they crawled inside!"

"I never see ladybugs outside in the winter," Bess said.

"And that guy from Pests R Best said he delivered ladybugs to River Heights," George said. "Maybe he delivered them to Gwendolyn and Carolyn."

"We have to question them!" Nancy decided.

"We don't know where they live," Bess said.

"We don't have to," Nancy said. "Gwendolyn and Carolyn are probably at the Lucky Ladybug Café right now."

"Doing what?" George asked.

"Cleaning out ladybugs," Nancy answered. "Their own ladybugs!"

CHAPTER TEN

Cupcake Comeback

Nancy, Bess, and George walked two blocks to Main Street. A Bug Busters truck was just pulling away from the Lucky Ladybug Cupcake Café.

"They're probably exterminators," George said.

"Poor ladybugs!" Bess sighed.

The Clue Crew quietly walked inside the store. Gwendolyn and Carolyn were inside scrubbing the counter and shelves. So was Trent. Gone were the perky cupcake-shaped baker hats. Instead they wore dreary brown hairnets.

"Sorry, girls," Carolyn said, still scrubbing. "No cupcakes today."

"Or ever," Gwendolyn grumbled as she sprayed the counter with disinfectant.

"We don't want cupcakes," Nancy said. "We want to ask you something."

"What do you want to know?" Gwendolyn asked.

"Did you ever order five hundred live ladybugs?" Nancy said.

"Why would we order live ladybugs?" Gwendolyn scoffed.

"That would be kind of weird," Carolyn admitted.

Nancy looked around for Trent. Where did he go? Suddenly Nancy spotted him through the back door. He was in the garden on his hands and knees, rummaging through the bushes!

As Nancy watched Trent, she remembered something. Something important!

"Mayor Strong told us that Trent was in the garden while he was sneaking cupcake bites," Nancy whispered to Bess and George. "Do you think Trent had something to do with the ladybugs?"

"There's only one way to find out," George whispered.

Trent's head was still in the bushes when Nancy, Bess, and George stepped outside.

"Hey, Trent," George said.

Trent was startled by George's voice. He pulled his head out of the bushes, but tangled his hair in a branch.

"Ow!" he cried.

"Sorry to sneak up on you," Nancy said. "But if you were looking for something, I think we already found it."

Trent yanked his hair free. "I wasn't looking for the ladybug jar," he said. "I was just—"

"Aha!" George cut in. "We never said the ladybugs came in a jar."

"How would you know about the jar, Trent?" Nancy asked. "Unless you were the one who ordered the ladybugs."

"Did you do it, Trent?" Bess asked.

Trent gulped and his shoulders drooped.

"Yeah, I did it," he said. "I ordered the

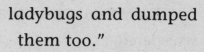

ladybugs and dumped them too."

"*You* did it?" Gwendolyn asked.

Nancy, Bess, and George turned to see the sisters standing in the garden.

"Why would you want to ruin our store, Trent?" Carolyn asked. "I thought we were a team."

Trent opened his mouth to speak, but nothing came out. So Nancy stepped forward and said, "Trent probably ordered the ladybugs for your garden."

"What for?" Gwendolyn asked, surprised.

"The Creature Teacher says some bugs are great at eating other bugs that eat flowers," Nancy explained.

"Ladybugs might be good for gardens too," Bess said.

Carolyn turned to her sister. "We did ask Trent to pick up a pesticide," she said.

"Something safe and natural," Gwendolyn agreed. "Because people would be eating cupcakes out here."

"There's nothing more natural than ladybugs," George said.

Trent shook his head as if he didn't get it.

"But I sprinkled the ladybugs around the bushes," Trent said. "How did they all end up inside the store?"

"The Creature Teacher says some bugs don't like the cold," Nancy said. "They probably crawled inside to get warm."

"And swarmed when the crowds came in," George added.

"I did leave the back door open that morning to let in fresh air," Trent groaned. "Instead I let in ladybugs. Boy, did I goof up!"

Nancy turned to see both sisters smiling.

"It was an honest mistake, Trent," Gwendolyn said.

"You wanted to help with those ladybugs," Carolyn said. "It's just too bad they weren't the lucky kind."

"Oh, yes they were!" Nancy said.

"What do you mean?" Gwendolyn asked.

"Mayor Strong really liked your cupcakes," Nancy explained. "He wants the Lucky Ladybug Cupcake Café to open again!"

"How's *that* for lucky?" George asked.

Gwendolyn, Carolyn, and Trent traded happy high fives. They then turned to Nancy, Bess, and George.

"How did you figure all this out?" Carolyn asked.

"We're detectives," Bess said.

"All in a day's work," George said with a shrug.

"Well, you girls make great detectives!" Gwendolyn said.

"And you make cool cupcakes," Nancy said with a grin.

Two weeks later spring had finally sprung—and the Lucky Ladybug Café was once again open for business. This time Mayor Strong was there for the grand opening. So were Olivia Chow and her brother, Lester.

"Are your cupcakes really here too, Olivia?" Nancy asked.

Olivia pointed proudly to some cupcakes on the counter. "Gwendolyn and Carolyn tasted my cupcakes," she said. "They liked them so much they decided to sell a few!"

"Try the grasshopper mint cupcakes," Lester said. "They rock."

"Grasshopper?" Bess gulped. "Do the cupcakes have real, live—"

"Bess, get over it," George cut in. "There are no more bugs here."

Buggy Wozniak pointed to a nearby wall. "Just one awesome bug *poster*!" he exclaimed.

Nancy looked at Buggy's new poster for the Bug Club. Instead of dung beetles and tarantulas it had butterflies and ladybugs.

Buggy was happy again. So was Olivia. But nobody was happier than the Clue Crew.

"Not only did we solve another case," Bess said as they joined the line for cupcakes. "We got our new cupcake café back."

"Are we lucky or what?" George said.

"That's for sure," Nancy said happily. "Thanks to a few good clues—and lots of lucky ladybugs!"

LADYBUG CUPCAKES

Ladybugs may be lucky, but these ladybug cup-cakes are totally *yummy*. And guess what? With a little help from an adult, they're super easy to make, too!

Ingredients

1 package chocolate cake or cupcake mix

1 container ready-to-spread white frosting

Red food coloring

Chocolate malt balls

Black jellybeans or chocolate chips

Black or brown shoestring licorice candy

Instructions

1. Have an adult help you bake the chocolate cupcakes.
2. Wait for cupcakes to cool.
3. Using the food coloring, tint white frosting red.
4. Spread and smooth bright red frosting on tops of cupcakes.
5. Stick a malt ball on the edge of the cupcake for the ladybug's head.
6. Cut a string of licorice to size, then lay it down the middle of the ladybug's back.
7. Dot jellybeans or chocolate chips on both sides of the licorice string.
8. Stick two small pieces of licorice string behind the malt ball head for the ladybug's antennae. Done!

Celebrate spring—or any season—with these cute-as-a-bug treats!

Break out your sleeping bag and best pajamas. . . . You're invited!

Sleepover Squad

❀ Collect them all! ❀